Toby Laughs Last

Toby Laughs Last

Jean Lemieux

Illustrated by Sophie Casson
Translated by Sarah Cummins

First Novels

Formac Publishing Company Limited
Halifax, Nova Scotia

Originally published as *Ma vie sans rire*
Text copyright © 2006 Sarah Cummins
Illustration copyright © Sophie Casson

Formac Publishing Company Limited recognizes the support of the
Province of Nova Scotia through the Department of Tourism, Culture and
Heritage. We acknowledge the financial support of the Government of
Canada through the Book Publishing Industry Development Program
(BPIDP) for our publishing activities.

Formac Publishing Company Limited acknowledges the support of the
Canada Council for the Arts for our publishing program.

Library and Archives Canada Cataloguing in Publication

Lemieux, Jean, 1954-
[Ma vie sans rire. English]
        Toby laughs last / Jean Lemieux ; illustrations by
        Sophie Casson ; translated by Sarah Cummins.

(First novels ; 59)
Translation of: Ma vie sans rire.
ISBN-10: 0-88780-720-8 (bound) ISBN-13: 978-0-88780-720-6 (bound)
ISBN-10: 0-88780-716-X (pbk.) ISBN-13: 978-0-88780-716-9 (pbk.)

        1. Emotions—Juvenile fiction. I. Casson, Sophie II.
        Cummins, Sarah III. Title. IV. Title: Ma vie sans rire.
        English. V. Series.

PS8573.E5427M313 2006   jC843'.54   C2006-904392-2

Formac Publishing Company Ltd.   Distributed in the United States by:
5502 Atlantic Street   Orca Book Publishers
Halifax, Nova Scotia, B3H 1G4   P.O. Box 468 Custer, WA
www.formac.ca   USA 98240-0468

Printed and bound in Canada

Table of Contents

1
Kite Problems

My name is Toby Omeranovic and I'm eight years old. I am a totally normal kid, except for just one thing: I ask a lot of *questions*.

For instance, why are there a *g* and an *h* in the word *through*? Is there anything behind the stars? Why do parents get to decide everything for their children?

There's no doubt about it. For me, questions are like a disease. My parents even bought me a dog to cure me of asking so many questions, or at least make me easier to put up with.

Sometimes I ask very complicated questions, but fortunately, I ask very simple ones, too.

For example: would a branch about as big around as my leg be able to support my weight?

***

It was a Saturday morning in May. The lilac bush in the Bainbridge-Babcocks' yard was in bloom.

My friend Marianne and I were heading to the city park about three blocks from my house. My dog Napoleon was trotting along with us, sniffing excitedly at all the smells of spring. The sun was shining, and a strong west wind was blowing through the city.

I was holding my new kite,
a beautiful V-shaped one I had bought
last summer, when we went on vacation
to the ocean. I was going to try flying it
for the very first time.

The park is called Isaac Newton
Park. To impress Marianne, I asked her
if she knew who Isaac Newton was.

"No," she answered. She didn't
seem impressed.

"Isaac Newton," I announced, "was
an English scientist of the seventeenth
century. He discovered the law of
universal gravitation."

Marianne said nothing, so I went on.

"Universal gravitation is what
causes things to fall. Newton got the
idea when he saw an apple fall in an
orchard. According to legend, the apple

fell on his head, but no one can prove that's true."

We walked to the middle of the park. I laid the kite on the ground, unrolled the string, and gave a little tug so the kite would rise.

For some reason, the kite didn't

seem very enthusiastic. Was it because
it had spent the winter in the attic?
It rose up a little, then

Isaac
Newton
Park

veered off to the left and dove to the ground.

I was not happy. I had told Marianne I had a fantastic kite, and now I couldn't even get it off the ground!

I adjusted the frame. I would get that kite to fly to the stars, or my name wasn't Toby Omeranovic! I tried again.

Hooray! This time, we had liftoff! The kite rose straight up into the sky. It was so high that I felt I was up there too, flying along with the sparrows and crows. Then it started veering to the left again and fell down and got stuck in a tree.

After trying fourteen times to free it, Marianne and I agreed that there was only one solution. Someone would have to go up there and get the kite unstuck. In order to do that, someone would have to climb the tree and crawl out on a branch. The branch looked to be about as big around as my leg.

It also looked to be about ten metres off the ground.

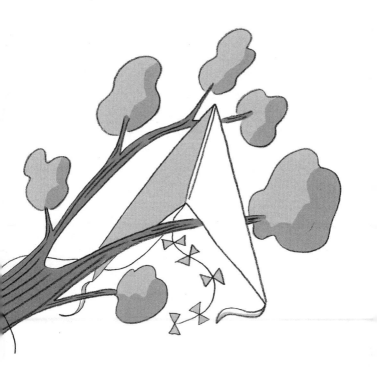

2
Trying to Impress

Two things explain what happened next: showing off and a fungus.

Normally, I would never try to climb such a tall tree to rescue a kite. I would be too scared.

This was not a normal time. My friend Marianne was there.

"The kite is too high up," she said. "There is no way *you* could climb up there."

That decided it. If anyone was brave enough, or crazy enough, to climb up that tree, it was me. Something — I don't know what — made my mouth say the following words:

"Ha! I've already climbed much taller trees!"

There was no going back after that. I wanted to impress Marianne. I wanted her to think that I was not afraid to climb ten metres up a tree.

The problem with wanting to impress someone is that once you've started, you have to go through with it. So I, Toby Omeranovic the Hero, walked over to the tree.

Napoleon started barking. He did not think this was a good idea. I grabbed the lowest branch and started to climb.

This is where the fungus comes in.

If I hadn't been trying so hard to impress Marianne, I might have noticed

that the tree that had trapped my kite was an American elm. I might also have noticed that this particular tree did not seem very healthy. The leaves on some of the branches had turned brown.

This was because of a fungus. There are two kinds of fungi: big ones and little ones. The big ones are called mushrooms, and they're the kind we eat. The little ones are the kind that eat trees, especially American elms.

The elm that I was climbing was not dead yet, but it was dying. I climbed higher, quaking from head to toe. Napoleon was worried and barked louder. I prayed that a grown-up would appear and order me to come down immediately. I would be delighted to obey.

But vanity kept me climbing. I was a hero. The kite was now only two metres away. I inched closer. Suddenly I heard a little cracking sound.

In less than a second, it turned into a big cracking sound.

And then, I had the answer to my question.

It was *no*. A branch of a diseased American elm, about as big around as my leg, cannot support my weight.

With a shriek that must have been heard at the North Pole, I obeyed Newton's law of universal gravitation. I fell.

Like an apple.

3
The Tunnel of Death

My book on the great inventors does not say what happened to the apple after it fell on Isaac Newton's head.

And I cannot tell you what happened after I crashed to the ground underneath the American elm.

I don't remember. The last thing I remember seeing was Marianne and Napoleon staring as I fell. Their eyes were as big as saucers and they were howling.

After that, I went into the tunnel of death.

Once I saw this TV program about

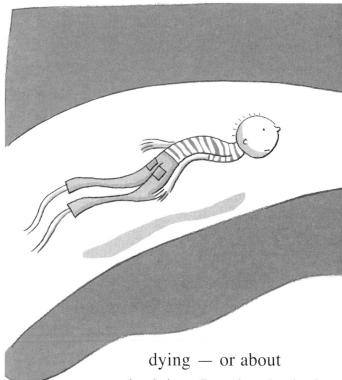

dying — or about
nearly dying. People who had
nearly died described what it was like.
Some had almost drowned. Others had
been in a car crash. There was even one
who was having his tonsils removed.

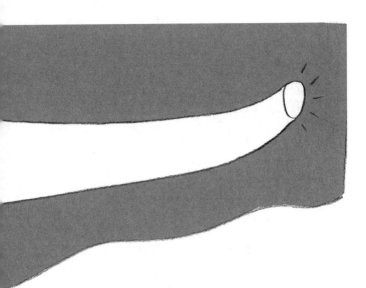

All of these people described the sensation of walking through a tunnel. There was a bright light at the end. They weren't in pain. They said it was almost a pleasant feeling.

Well, I, Toby Omeranovic, can tell you that this tunnel of death exists. I passed through it.

The first thing I can remember from

after my fall was being in a big white tube. A woman was speaking, very softly, telling me not to move. I was so happy to hear a sound, any sound, that I fell back asleep.

When I woke up, I was surrounded by a whole bunch of people in blue pyjamas. My neck was held in a kind of clamp, so that I couldn't turn my head. There was a needle stuck in my right arm.

I was just coming out of the big white tube, where a computer had taken pictures of my body.

The people in pyjamas put me on a gurney and pushed me down a hallway. And then — I'll remember this my whole life — Mom was there.

I felt her warm hand holding mine.

I needed that, because I felt so cold inside. I felt very weak, as if I had had the flu for two and a half months.

I felt like sleeping. Just sleeping forever, because it was so tiring to keep on breathing, and holding my eyes open, and living. And my left leg hurt a lot.

But Mom was there. She stroked my cheek as the gurney rolled along.

"Don't worry, Toby," she reassured me. "We'll get your kite back for you."

Of course, it was a joke. My mom is indestructible. If she was teasing me, that meant nothing bad could happen.

"You're going to be all right," she told me.

She let go of my hand. I was wheeled into the operating room. There was a big circle of light above my head. If Mom said I was going to be all right, then I was going to be all right.

I fell asleep again. It felt good.

***

When I woke up, my left leg was in a cast. My left arm was in a cast. A tube was coming out of my side. It was attached to a machine that made bubbles. I had a huge bandage over my stomach.

I was in intensive care, but I felt much better. I didn't feel cold inside anymore. I didn't feel like sleeping.

Yippee! Hooray! Callooh! Callay! I was *alive*!

My parents came in and they explained everything to me. I had a fractured femur, a fractured elbow, fractured ribs, and blood in my lungs.

That's what I *had*. What I no longer had was a *spleen*.

"What's a spleen?"

"It's an organ, kind of like a sponge, near your stomach on the upper left. They took your spleen out because it was bleeding."

"What does a spleen do?"

"Not much. You can do without it, no problem."

So I used to have a kind of sponge inside that didn't do anything. Weird! I always thought that every part of me was good for something.

Spleen. The word sounded kind of funny, and I was so happy to be alive that I started to laugh. *Ha-ha! Hee-hee!*

I regretted it immediately. My left

side hurt so much that I almost started
to cry.

I was discovering the effects of my
accident.

I couldn't laugh any more!

It wasn't funny at all.

4
An Empty Jar
of Peanut Butter

Two days after my operation, the surgeon, Dr. Bigelow, announced that he could now remove the tube from my lungs.

"Afterwards, will I be able to laugh?" I asked.

The young interns that were doing the rounds with him all chuckled. I kept my eyes on Dr. Bigelow. I liked him. For one thing, he had absolutely no sense of humour. For another, he talked to me as if I were a grown-up.

"Not for a few more days," he told

me. "When you laugh, the muscles in your thorax make your rib cage move, and that's what hurts."

He pulled the tube out. *Shlook!* It hurt, but not as much as I thought it would.

"However, as a doctor, I can assure you that you can survive for two or three weeks without laughing."

The interns all smiled again.
But Dr. Bigelow's face was serious.
Maybe he *did* have a sense of humour,
the kind that makes you laugh *inside*.

He pointed his finger at me.

"On the other hand," he said
seriously, "if you go for more than
three weeks without laughing, the
health risks are very serious indeed."

Then he was gone in a flash,
the same way he had come. I was left
all alone with my questions. What did
he mean — 'serious health risks'?

It must be more of that *inside* humour.

***

Now that I wasn't attached by a tube
to anything, I could move around in a

wheelchair. When I wasn't getting treatment, I roamed the hospital corridors or went to watch television in the lounge. When the weather was nice, I went outside to the veranda.

The hospital was a very serious place, full of very sick patients and very busy nurses. There were few reasons to laugh. That was fine, since I didn't feel like laughing. My left side still hurt too much.

Dr. Bigelow came by to see me every morning. I thought of a lot of questions to ask him. Is the spleen really a useless organ? What will happen to me if I go for more than three weeks without laughing? Will I be invaded by a fungus, like the American elm?

I don't know if the accident had made me shy or just too weak, but I never dared to ask him these questions.

Four days later, on a Thursday, Dr. Bigelow said that I was well enough to go home.

"When can he go back to school?" my mom asked.

"Not for another ten days. Our young friend needs to get his strength back."

Another ten days! I should have been jumping for joy at the idea of being on holiday at home. But I felt nothing. I wasn't happy. I wasn't unhappy. I was like an empty jar of peanut butter. Not creamy, not crunchy.

***

Napoleon was waiting faithfully for me at home. While I had been in hospital, he had spent almost all his time looking out the window, waiting for my return.

When Dad laid me down on the sofa, Napoleon jumped up onto me and began to lick my face.

"Ow! Ow!"

Just try explaining to a Neapolitan terrier that his master's femur, elbow, and ribs — in fact the whole left side — is as sore as a marmot with the mumps!

But Napoleon was a smart dog, and he understood that he had to be careful with me. He lay down at my side and stared at me in adoration, as if I were Isaac Newton in person.

Mom tucked me in comfortably on the sofa. She brought me pillows, my favourite blanket, and some comic books to read.

I leafed through them, then I gave them back to her.

"Could you take these back to my room, please? I'm afraid they'll make me laugh. I don't want anything inside to come undone."

"Toby! Nothing's going to come undone!"

"It might! Did you tell the *others?*"

The others were my brother Will and my sister Emily. I knew what they were like. They would try to make me laugh. Mom said she had told them not to tease me, but I couldn't be sure they wouldn't.

Mom took the books, sat down, and laid her hand on my forehead. She looked worried.

"It's a good thing you're back home, Toby. You're not your usual self."

Before she left the room, I asked, as a last favour, if she would please bring me the dictionary.

5
Spleenless

It was just as I suspected. The spleen does have a purpose. I found this definition in the dictionary:

spleen: a highly vascular ductless organ near the stomach or intestine of most vertebrates, concerned with final destruction of blood cells, storage of blood, and production of lymphocytes.

And that wasn't all! *Spleen* also means "lowness of spirits, moroseness, ill temper, spite." No wonder I felt so bad!

Then Mom brought me the big dictionary, the one that you have to read with a magnifying glass. This is what I found:

Regarded as the seat of laughter or mirth.

One of the old quotations given was: "Such matter as will make you laugh your fill, if you have a laughing spleene."

Now I understood. I couldn't laugh my fill, because I

didn't have a laughing spleen. I no
longer had *any* spleen. Dr. Bigelow and
my parents had lied to me! They had
said I would be as good
as new, but they
didn't mention that I

would be handicapped because I had no spleen.

I was angry and I felt like crying.

"Napoleon, what will I do if I can't laugh anymore? A life without laughter would be like having winter all year round."

But before Napoleon could do anything to cheer me up, Catherine Bainbridge-Babcock, my neighbour and friend since forever, walked into the living room. In her hand she held a bouquet of lilacs.

She seemed shocked to see the state I was in. Lying on the sofa, pale and sickly, my arm and leg covered in casts, I must have looked like a half a mummy.

"Your mom asked me to bring your

homework over."

Beebee — that's her nickname — came over to the sofa, and Napoleon started to growl.

"What's with him?" she asked.

"I don't know. He thinks he's guarding me."

I took the flowers and buried my nose in them. Mmmm ... they smelled good. They tickled my nostrils a little bit, and all of a sudden —

"*Atchooo!*"

Ow! It felt like I had been stabbed in the side. I had forgotten about my allergies!

Beebee is not like Dr. Bigelow. Her sense of humour is on the outside. She began to laugh and laugh, and she couldn't stop. She must have thought it was very funny to see a spleenless handicapped person wincing in pain!

I think I would have thought it was funny too, before my accident. Now I didn't think it was funny at all. I was

angry. I thrust the bouquet at Beebee, who was still doubled over with giggles.

"Thank you for the flowers and for bringing my homework. Now I would like you to go. I'm tired."

Beebee stopped laughing and looked at me sorrowfully, as if I had cancer or, worse yet, the chicken pox. She left, shaking her head sadly.

Half an hour later, my eleven-year-old brother Will got home from school. Mom told him to handle me with kid gloves, but he soon barged into the living room.

He was walking stiffly and looked very serious. At my feet, Napoleon growled again. He could smell danger.

Will sat down at the other end of the sofa.

"How's it going, bro'?"

I said it was going fine. Then,
without warning, Will made his very
worst face at me, the one where he
twists his neck, screws up his mouth,
and crosses his eyes.

Nothing happened inside me.
I gazed at my brother making an idiot
of himself, and I didn't have the

slightest desire to laugh. Will got worried.

"Are you sure you're all right?"

A big lump of unhappiness rose up in my throat and I didn't know what to do. I couldn't breathe, and my eyes filled with tears.

"Go away!" I cried. "Leave me alone!"

Will left. Naturally, he told Mom everything, and soon enough she came into the living room, too. She sat down next to me and stroked my hair.

"What's up, Toby?"

Once in a while, I can keep something from my mom, but never when she's stroking my hair. She knows it, too.

"Since they took out my spleen,

I can't laugh anymore."

"But Dr. Bigelow explained it to you. Your ribs hurt when you laugh."

"You don't understand! I don't even *feel* like laughing anymore!"

And I told her about the spleen being the seat of laughter and mirth, and about the lump in my throat. Mom listened patiently, still stroking my hair.

I told her about everything that had made me feel bad ever since I fell out of that American elm.

"You had a very serious accident, Toby," she said simply, when I had finished. "You need *rest*. In a few days, you'll feel a lot better."

6
The Door to Laughter

Resting, I guess, just means not doing very much. That suited me fine. There was no one I wanted to see. Nothing I wanted to do.

I asked my mom to close the doors and the windows and to draw the blinds. I wanted to be alone, lying on the sofa in the dark, with just the television to keep me company.

Friday, Saturday, Sunday ... I rested in the dark like this for the whole weekend.

I watched cartoons, the parliamentary channel, curling —

anything. I slept badly and I had
nightmares. I was always falling out of
that tree again, over and over, all the
time. I went through the tunnel of
death. Isaac Newton appeared, wearing
my brother's hockey jersey, and made
faces at me.

My friends came by to ask how I was doing. Mom didn't let them come into the living room. Marianne sent me a get-well card.

I didn't feel like laughing, but at least my ribs didn't hurt anymore. I felt safe.

But while lying in the dark feeling safe might be restful, it is also *boring*. I had time to think. I thought about my accident, and I figured that it wasn't fair.

Why did this have to happen to me, Toby Omeranovic? I felt very sorry for myself, with my broken bones and missing spleen! I felt like I would never get well. I would have to lie on the sofa in the dark until I died.

On Sunday evening, I tried laughing a little bit. *Hee-hee! Ha-ha!* It didn't hurt as much, but it wasn't any fun either.

Having all the doors and windows closed didn't make my laugh come back. Maybe laughter is just like a door in your head. If I opened the door, all the dark ideas would go out and happiness could come in.

I was suddenly very worried. My laughter door was stuck! I wanted to start really living again, even if my ribs hurt.

I called out to my mom. I didn't even have to speak. She understood me.

"Still not feeling great, Toby?" she asked. "Tomorrow we'll go see Dr. Bigelow. I'm sure he can do something about those lumps in your throat."

***

The next morning, after another night
of nightmares, Mom and
I walked into
Dr. Bigelow's office.
What a surprise!

He had his arm in a cast!

I felt a kind of tickling in my nose. I didn't think it was my allergies. No, I wasn't dreaming. I almost felt like laughing.

Dr. Bigelow also had a black eye and scrapes on his forehead! It was funny. It did me a lot of good to see him like that.

"Ahem," he cleared his throat. "As you can see, my friend Toby, a broken arm can happen to anyone. In my case, I can't blame it on a kite. The culprit was a fire truck."

"Were you run over by a fire truck?" I gasped.

"No, I slipped on a toy fire truck that was sitting on the basement steps. And now I won't be able to operate for six weeks! Well, what brings you here, Toby?"

Mom told him how I had been. I never laughed any more. I had nightmares. I spent all my time alone in the dark watching curling. And my laughter door was stuck and I had lumps in my throat.

Surgeons are kind of like mechanics. They fix the parts of the body that aren't working right, or take them out.

Dr. Bigelow asked me a lot of questions to figure out my problem. Then he examined my ribs and my scar.

"It looks good, Toby. You're *almost* well. If you haven't started laughing again, it's not because of your spleen. It's due to shock."

Shock? Dr. Bigelow explained.

The problem wasn't inside my body, but inside my head. In my feelings.

It's as if the accident had banged me hard on the head. I was so badly hurt,

and so afraid, that my head was still ringing like a bell. My body was tired and my thoughts were confused. I felt sad, although I didn't know why.

"How can I get the bell to stop ringing?"

"You have to talk about your feelings. And not spend all your time alone in the dark. Today, you're going to start going out again. And in two days, back to school."

"Two days?"

The worst of it was, I was almost happy at the thought.

***

I had never been to the park in a wheelchair before. It was fun.

Especially when my dad was pushing the chair and all my friends were there.

Everyone had come: Beebee, Sigi, Marianne, and the new kid in the neighbourhood, Merlin Higginbottom-Campari. And Napoleon was trotting along beside me, wagging his tail at warp speed.

Marianne was carrying my kite. What a nice surprise! Dad had repaired it while I was in the hospital.

I hadn't laughed yet. But I was smiling a lot.

Inside the park, we stopped at the foot of the tree that had caused me so much grief. I looked way, way up at the broken branch, ten metres above me.

I turned to Marianne.

"Did I really climb up there?"

"You did. I was so afraid for you.
I thought you were going to die."

Suddenly, we were all very serious.
The lump got stuck in my throat again.
But it didn't last long. Now I knew it
was only the effect of shock.

Then my father broke the spell.

"Let's see how this kite flies.
Check out my technique."

Dad turned the kite into the wind and jerked at the string. The kite shot into the sky. It was flying very well, better than the last time, anyway. Then it veered off to the left and started to dive. Dad tried hard to keep it up, but it landed in a birch tree.

"Ho-ho! Hee-hee! Ha-ha!"

Spleen or no spleen, I laughed my head off.

More new novels in the *First Novels Series*!

Maddie's Big Test
Louise Leblanc
Illustrated by Marie-Louise Gay
Translated by Sarah Cummins

It's time for the big math test at school, and Maddie's worried. Then her friends show her how she can cheat, and Maddie doesn't need to study any more. Cheating has to be a better plan than wasting time studying for a test — right?

In this story, Maddie learns that taking the time to study can be a lot simpler than cheating.

Toni Biscotti's Magic Trick
Caroline Merola
Illustrated by Caroline Merola
Translated by Sarah Cummins

Toni Biscotti is shy — really shy. Yet for some reason she has signed up to perform at the school concert. Will she be able to put together an act good enough to impress Marco Pirelli? Toni can't dance, can't sing, can't play a musical instrument — what on earth is she going to do? Perhaps her grandmother the sorcerer can help her out...

In this story, Toni discovers that it's not really so hard to make magic happen.

Formac Publishing Company Limited
5502 Atlantic Street
Halifax, Nova Scotia B3H 1G4

Orders: 1-800-565-1975
Fax: 902-425-0166
www.formac.ca